"Derek McC

writer ~~and a great discovery.~~"
—Dennis Cooper

"Derek McCormack's among the
best writers in the country."
—Bill Richardson, *National Post*

"Anyone interested in the more wicked,
crafty and inventive forms of Canadian
writing would be well advised
to spend time with McCormack."
—Philip Marchand, *The Toronto Star*

"McCormack is an amazing stylist,
producing incredibly tight pages
of deceptively simple-seeming
James Ellroy-like sentences."
—Hal Niedzviecki and Darren Wershler-Henry,
The Original Canadian City Dweller's Almanac

"McCormack's an evil little blessing."
—Bert Archer, *NOW*

THE HAUNTED HILLBILLY

DEREK McCORMACK

MISFIT

Published by ECW PRESS
2120 Queen Street East, Suite 200, Toronto, Ontario, Canada M4E 1E2

NATIONAL LIBRARY OF CANADA CATALOGUING IN PUBLICATION DATA

McCormack, Derek, 1969-
The haunted hillbilly / Derek McCormack.

ISBN 1-55022-610-X

I. Title.

PS8575.C664H39 2003   C813'.54   C2003-902195-5
PR9199.3.M295H39 2003

Editor: Michael Holmes / a misFit book
Cover illustration and interior design: Ian Phillips
Printing: Transcontinental

This book is set in Tribute

ECW acknowledges the support of the Government of Canada through the Book Publishing Industy Development Program. Canada The author and publisher acknowledge the kind support of the Toronto Arts Council, the Ontario Arts Council, and the Canada Council.

Thanks to *Brick: A Literary Journal*, *Broken Pencil*, Coach House Books, Gutter Press, and Pedlar Press.

Thanks to Hilary McMahon and WCA. To Jack David, Michael Holmes, and ECW PRESS. And to Carey Low and Canadian Manda Group. Special thanks to Tony Burgess, Mona Gupta, Jason McBride, Ian Phillips, Ken Sparling, and the McCormack family—Cynthia, Melissa, and Murray.

Sections of *The Haunted Hillbilly* were previously published. Thanks to the editors of the following: <www.lowblueflame.com>; *The Notebooks: Interviews and New Fiction from Contemporary Writers* (Doubleday Canada, 2002); and *Taddle Creek*. Chapters of *The Haunted Hillbilly* first appeared in *Western Suit* (pas de chance, 2001).

DISTRIBUTION
CANADA: Jaguar Book Group, 100 Armstrong Avenue, Georgetown, ON L7G 5S4

PRINTED AND BOUND IN CANADA

ECW PRESS
ecwpress.com

CHAPTER ONE

{H}ank tears off his blindfold.

"Surprise!" Audrey's holding a suit.

"Aud, it's beautiful." It's brown. Scraps scattered around her sewing room. He slips the blazer on.

She shows him the pattern. Western Suit, it says. Her Singer's still hot. "I've been working on it for weeks."

He throws his arms out. "Look at me!"

She looks at him. Kisses him. He kisses back. They drop to their knees, roll on the floor.

Pattern pieces. Straight sleeve. Straight legs.

The blindfold—a sock.

—✦—

A dime store. Shirts a dollar.

Hank's in Men's. "I'm looking for something to go with my suit," he says.

The clerk pulls out possibilities. White, off-white, cream, tan, chocolate. A tan check. The whole store smells like Pets.

Hank doesn't know. "Maybe I should wait for Audrey."

—✦—

The sun's practically set. Windows are mirrors. Hank squints into shops, sees himself.

He clops up Printer's Alley. It's deserted. Dumpsters and dog shit. A bright black blur swooping down from the sky.

A bat.

Smack. Hits Hank square on the head. He falls ass-backward, sprawls on cement. That's when he sees it. In the second-story window of a false-fronted store. It sparkles. A shirt.

⟞⟝

Fabrics abound. Cottons the colours of comics. It's like nowhere Hank's been.

I appear.

"I'm Nudie," I say. I look not unlike Mandrake. Mandrake moustache. Mandrake suit. I bow. "Welcome to my atelier."

Hank holds his head. "A tell you what?" he says. He's bleeding. He leans against a radiator. It's bolts of silver lamé.

"I'll pour you a toddy."

"Don't touch the stuff. Not anymore." He limps to a couch. Drops. A gorilla beside him. He looks at it. At me. Woozy.

"It's a costume," I say. "Created for a sideshow." The fur's fake. Yugoslavian. The best fake gorilla fur always is. "I'm a carnival couturier."

Hank's blank.

"Let me illustrate."

CHAPTER TWO

ank climbs from my Cadillac.

"This," I say, "is my trunk show."

"What?" He cups his ear to hear. There are klaxons.

And whistles. And bells. It's a carnival. The ground's dressed in sawdust. Sawdust dyed pink. Fog is fake.

"It's a horseshoe," I say. Games in the front-end. Rides midway down the midway. The Haunted House screams. Nobody in it. Nobody around. Just Hank and I.

"Can I?" He runs into the funhouse. The hall of mirrors. Glass smeared with snot and blood. He steps into the exit. A rolling barrel. He falls, tries to get up. The Human Laundry, it's called.

"Bad idea," he says, limping back.

I guide him deep into the back-end. Sideshow banners break. "Do you like naked ladies?"

—🦇—

Hank ducks into a tent. I follow. Canvas cooks. The P.A. crackles. Oompah tunes. Lights dim.

Girls grind onstage. They're nude. Or they might be. A curtain of black gauze conceals them. "This is how I began," I say. "Making their costumes."

Hank leans in. "What costumes?"

"Nude-toned suits," I say.

"It's so frustrating!" he laughs. "I feel like a widow!"

—🦇—

"To sew what?" Hank says.

"Tussaud," I say. "The greatest wax museum in the world. Besides this one." Wax statues pose artistically. Hank walks up to a fellow in animal skins.

"Genghis Khan," I say. The exhibit: World's Worst Criminals. Jack the Ripper in a swallow-tail coat. Benedict Arnold in a powdered wig. I thought of everything.

Hank stares down Billy the Kid. Billy's face has been hairsprayed. To repel dust. Suit fireproofed with wax.

Hank touches Billy's hand. Leaves fingerprints.

The seal boy waves. A fin.

"Good day," I say. It's the freak show.

A fat lady waddles onstage. Half a ton. Flesh

cuffs over shoes. Her pinafore's sizes too small.

"It fits great, Mr. Nudie."

"Glad to hear it."

Behind a canvas curtain, the blowoff. There's a mermaid: a fish tail I stitched to the body of a gopher. There's a Tasmanian devil: a monkey head I stitched to a stuffed cat.

A row of jars. In each jar a baby. A baby with two heads. A baby with a tail. A baby with frog flippers.

"God made those," I say.

❧

Salad fork, supper fork, soup spoon. Audrey straightens settings. Her special silver. She adds grains of rice to the salt. Rice stops salt from clumping.

The night's close. She steps onto the stoop. The sky's very Ray Bradbury. A weird wind.

Clouds mean business.

"Where in hell is he?"

The popcorn's really chicken corn. Butter's
oleo. A pound of sugar spins fifty cotton candy
cones. Candy apples bruised.

"Anything you want, Hank," I say. "It's on me."

"That's awful nice of you, Mr. Nudie." Hank
gets a banana dipped in chocolate. It drips.
"Darn," he says, rubs it into his wool.

I cock an eyebrow.

"I'm supposed to wear this on the Opry."

I cock the other eyebrow. "That? On the
Opry? I think not.

"Firstly, it's too heavy. The spotlights will
cook you. You'll be swimming in sweat.

"Secondly, you'll disappear into the
background. That fabric is beyond bland. It

belongs on an amplifier. You'll look like an amp.

"Thirdly, it's amateurish. Does Eddy Arnold wear homemade clothes? Does Roy Acuff's wife sew suits?"

I pluck a cigarette. My lighter's a pistol. I pull the trigger. "If I've offended you, I apologize." My face in smoke. "It's simply my professional opinion. Dress as you see fit."

Hank says nothing.

"Can I bum one?" Hank says.

⁂

Sailors, flappers, clowns. The shack's stacked with kewpie dolls. Hula girls with feather skirts.

"You want something special," I say. "Something that stands out. That no one's ever seen before. That says: I'm a star. I belong."

I hand him a kewpie. A cowboy. Purple shirt. Orange bandanna. Cherry chaps. Eyes airbrushed. But not well. One eye on his cheek.

"Chalkware," I say. "From the German. It's plaster of Paris. Costs pennies to make. Put it behind a carnival game, it's flash. Marks play till they win. Spend hundreds.

"That's what I'll make you. A kewpie doll. Flash."

———

"Look!" Hank says.

"It's purple," Audrey says. The shirt's satin, not sateen. "It won't go with your suit."

"That's the thing, Aud. He said he'd make all my clothes for free. But I can only wear his clothes. It's a whatchamacallit. A deal."

She turns it inside-out. Seams are seamless. Slip stitches like she's never seen. She measures the arms. They're different lengths. She measures the cuffs. They're different, too.

"It's beautiful," she says. "I can't compete."

"It's not a competition." He puts it on. It hugs him back. "See? I'm a kewpie doll. You know, like at carnivals?" He claps. "You've got to see this."

"You're lost," Audrey says.

Hank shakes his head. "I could've sworn."

They're standing at the side of a road. Jalopy sputters. Exhaust clings to their clothes.

"It was right off Demonbreun." He steps into a field. Manure browns his shoes. "There were rides. Games. Everything."

She smells dung. Sees a field ribbed like boot-treads. A farmer far out. A bony mule pulling a buzzard plow.

CHAPTER THREE

Guano, the sack says. Bat shit.

I slop some into a hair sieve. Pile broom brush on top. Set it aflame. It burns yellow with blue.

I douse it. Water drains through horse cloth, into a beaker. I boil it down to ash.

And crystals.

～～

I act distracted.

"It was just gone," Hank says.

"Midways are mysterious," I say. "Fly-by-night."

"Tell that to my wife." He's in the atelier for aperitifs.

I hoist a wineglass. I'm drinking red, from Graves. "To the Grand Ole Opry—the Hillbilly Big Top!"

He toasts me with tomato juice. "Ouch," he says, sipping. The rim of his goblet's crusted with crystals. Saltpeter. A bat byproduct. "The salt's sharp."

"Drink," I say.

⸻

"Hard day?" Audrey says.

Hank sinks onto the sofa. "Long," he says. "Nudie measured me thirty ways."

Audrey rubs Hank's shoulders. Slips her hands under his tee. His body more Marvel than

EC. She licks an ear. "I can help," she says.

"Maybe later," he says. "I'm thirsty."

◆━━

She tongues the shaft.

He lies still.

The dart of skin below the head. The slit, big as a buttonhole.

He sits up in bed. Soft. "I'm sorry," he says. "I don't know what's wrong."

◆━━

"Already?" Audrey says.

"Big day," Hank says, drooling toothpaste. "Nudie's doing my feet. He's got this X-ray machine."

Shower steam. The curtain draws back. Audrey's voluptuous enough. "Don't you want to stay a spell?"

Hank spits. "I already showered."

···

"Who is she?" Audrey whispers. "What's her name?" She peers through the living room drapes. Hank's standing in the road. There are no sidewalks in this Nashvillain neighbourhood.

Hank boards a bus. Downtown's that way. Audrey staggers through the house. Confronts the closet. Sniffs Hank's new shirt. It tells her nothing.

She wipes her eyes on the shirt. Tears bead. On the label a line drawing. A woman. Nude. The woman's straddling a snake fence, twirling a lasso. The noose a word balloon: Design by Nudie.

Of course, Audrey thinks.

···

Audrey climbs cockeyed steps. Her shadow

bigger than her.

She lets herself in. It's shadowy. Shapes hanging from hooks. Patterns. That one's Hank's leg. That one's his neck. No. It's a record sleeve. Hank's song drifts.

There's a judy. Hank's body. If he didn't have a head or arms. If his skin were horsehair. A steel rod up his butt.

She picks up lasts. They've been filed and chipped and sanded. There are toes and toenails. Arches. A plantar wart on the left heel. Hank's feet, only beech.

She shudders. Goose pimples are Ben Day dots.

There I am.

"Thank God," she sighs. "You're a man."

I smile. Hair slicked back. Vampire-style. "You must be Angela. Hank speaks of you often."

"I'm Audrey. Hank's wife. Who's Angela?"

"Hank has a wife?"

She flees. I turn to Hank's judy. Stroke
stumps. Lick chest. Stomach. My tongue brown,
furred with pile.

⸺⊷⸺

"I swear to you," Hank says.

Audrey's at her vanity, brushing her hair.

"There is no Angela. Nudie got confused."

Audrey rises. Walks to the bed. Throws Hank
a pillow. He sleeps on the sofa. He can't sleep.
Upholstery itches. Buttons devil.

⸺⊷⸺

Hank hides behind a screen.

"It's a mock-up," I say. "An *étoile*, as we
couturiers say. To see how the fabric will hang."

Hank steps out. The suit's organza. It looks
invisible. The ghost of a suit. Materialized.

24

I kneel behind, pretend to pin a cuff. His generous ass. I can taste it. His underwear no-names. Elastic slack. "I whipped up some shorts for you, Hank," I say, drawing a deep breath. "I sewed some for Audrey, too."

He snorts. "Now you remember her name."

I step into a back room. His shorts are boxers. Banjo bottoms. Hers I dust with saltpeter.

"They're lovely." Audrey fingers her panties, the monogram. "Are you sure they're not Angela's?"

"Don't say that." Hank kneels. Rubs her calves. Kisses her knees.

She parts them a hair.

He lifts her nightie. His head is underneath. He licks. Her panties taste of pee. And Cheer.

"Hank?" Audrey moans. "Are you hard?"

He half lies. He's half-hard. They fall into bed.

Fuck clothed. A button jams an eyelet. The tongue of his belt cold against her leg.

꽃

Back in the dime store. Parakeets talk shop.

Audrey leafs through patterns. Vogue, Butterick, McCall's. What does the wife of an Opry star wear?

Simplicity. Number 2066. She bends for a drawer. Yelps.

She goes to the basement. Stiffly. Sweat soaks her stockings. Sweat or blood. Skin cracks. She grabs a saleswoman. "Is there a change room?"

A saleswoman: "In Hardware?"

In the stall of a washroom, Audrey pulls down her panties. Her crotch splotchy. Future blisters.

꽃

I drop a magnet. Stray pins attack.

"The panties worked like a charm," Hank says.

"So glad." I chalk a sleeve. Tailor's chalk disappears when wet. A clothes steamer steams like a horse in cold.

It's the final fitting. Hank in magenta. More suits behind. Jade, scarlet, aquamarine. "Maybe you could make more clothes for Audrey," he says.

The door. Audrey. Grabs the first thing she sees: my muse, the cowboy kewpie. She pitches it. It hits the wall, cracks in three. Hat. Torso. Batwing chaps.

"You gave me the clap!" she says.

"What?" he says. "You have the clap?"

I slip into the back. Pick up the telephone. Tulane Hotel. "I'd like to book a room."

CHAPTER FOUR

ank takes a horse pill. Penicillin. Just in case. "I don't have the clap," he says. "Where would I get the clap?" He strips to gotchies. Sheets are short. The pillow's broken. The hotel sign a stir stick. Neon. Red spills in.

Hank shuts his eyes. Pictures Audrey in their bed. Audrey with another man. Two men. He punches his mattress. Fumbles for the phone, which is black.

"Room service?"

I knock. No answer.

It's nearly noon. I press an ear to the door. From my pocket I pull a stitch ripper. Slip it in the keyhole. Click.

I slip in. The room's a shambles. The radio's on. Hank's on it. Bedding strewn like splatter sheets.

Hank is in the bathroom. Head in the toilet. American Standard. The bowl full of gin. Bathtub full of empties. He moans. Help me. Or maybe, Audrey.

"Audrey's gone. She doesn't love you." I pop pills in his mouth.

In a flash he's up. "I'm up, I'm up."

"Get undressed."

Off comes his undershirt. His underpants. His ass round as a food dome. Smooth as silver plate.

"Put this on." I unzip a garment bag.

"Whoa." He teeters like a paper doll. "What

did you do?"

"I flashed it up." The blazer's ablaze. Sleeves studded with musical bars. Staffs are sequins. Notes are glass beads. A treble clef is scores of rhinestones.

⚜

"I feel dumb." Hank sinks into his seat. His suit tears the interior.

"Remember," I say. "You're flash. If you want to be a star, you've got to dress like a star. Now what do you want?"

I steer down the alley behind the Ryman Auditorium. The Ryman used to be a church. Hank climbs out. I park by Skull's Rainbow Room.

I tune the radio to WSM. Their needle towers over Nashville.

Their needle, I think, is no match for mine.

I laugh in block letters.

◆

Auditorium, the door says.

Hank sees: Audreytorium. He steps inside.

Clodhoppers everywhere.

He passes Stringbean. Stringbean's in jeans.
Roy Acuff in an off-the-rack three-piece. Hank
Snow in a string tie with Navaho slide. Minnie
Pearl's Minnie Pearl.

Ernest Tubb comes up. His suit's Sears. "Hey,
kid," he says. "How many batteries does your
suit take?" He laughs till he coughs.

Hank reaches for his boot. A flask hidden.

◆

The Opry throbs. Pews are packed. Standees
in the nosebleeds.

"We've got a real nice treat for you tonight,"

says Judge Roy Hay. He's in black tie. "His first time on the Grand Ole Opry. Let's give him a big down-home hand!"

Hank steps out. A gasp goes up. His suit's starry. Spotlights bend off his blazer. He sings his song. The one on his suit. About being blue.

The place goes ape. Folks hoot. Folks holler. Folks sweat. Work pants reek of dung. House-dresses cling. One-note perfumes. Radio Girl. Vogue.

In the wings the Judge gestures. "Again!" he mouths.

Hank goes again. The crowd encores again.

Nine encores later. Even the curtain is ruffled.

Where's Nudie? Hank thinks.

◆

"Little punk," Tubb says. He storms up the alley toward Skull's. The air's staticky. His suit staticky. The seat's shiny. "Nobody upstages Ernest Tubb!"

Thunder. Lilac sheets of lightning. The night engrossing ink.

A bat makes a moustache on the moon.

Audrey's in red panties.

Those aren't panties. They're blisters.

She holds a sewing needle in the flame of her kitchen range. It's a sharp, stainless steel. It gets red hot. She shoves it in a blister. Gasps. The needle hisses. The doorbell rings.

She squeezes. The blister bleeds. Pus. Iodine makes it angrier. She bandages it. The doorbell rings again. "For Christ's sake." She throws on her robe, limps to the door.

It's some lady. "Is Hank home?"

The lawn's full of fans.

"Tell Hank we love him!" a lady yells.

"I'll tell him!" Audrey says. "Right after I cut off his balls!"

A bat skins by. Marigolds scare mosquitoes.

Hank strides through a honky-tonk. Sawdust floors. Under each table a tray of kitty litter. To puke in.

He straddles a stool. Shining. He's still in his spangly suit. "Rum and Coke," he says.

He downs it. "To the Opry!"

He gets another. "To success!" He toasts till he's toasted. Couples reel on the dance floor. Wood planks laid over horsehair. Horsehair makes wood springy.

"In the shower!" Hank yells from the shower.

I move through his room. His scarf a Q on the carpet. His suit a glittering pile. Steeped in smoke. Cigarette scorch on a sleeve. "Did you have a good night?" I say.

"Quiet." Hank comes out. Steaming. He towels off. Clothes on his bed. A new suit. Sequinned with cattle brands. The running pitchfork. The sleeping coffin. Sundry slashes. "What's this for?"

"Interviews," I say. "Everyone wants the Opry's new star. *TIME. LIFE.* And another. *Hillbilly Fan*, I believe."

"That's my favourite!"

"Good. Here are your answers."

"What?" A typed sheet. He reads. "'I'll be taking a few days off. Going to Texas. For some serious R & R.'" He looks at me. "Am I really going to Texas?"

"No," I say.

🦇

Hank's strapped to a gurney.

"Gin?" the doctor says. He shuts Hank's nostrils with a clothespin. Puts a funnel in his mouth. Pours gin.

Hank gulps, then gulps air.

The doctor's old. He looks like Alfred. Batman's butler. He unsheathes a hypodermic, fills it. Something blue. He sticks it in Hank's arm.

Hank's eyes spin. He pukes. Gin. And what remains of a western. Sandwich.

Hank blacks out.

◂▸

The room's private. I'm by the dresser. "Sweet dreams?"

Hank shakes his head. Or vice-versa? Teeth chatter like novelty teeth. Lips, gown, hospital bracelet—hypothermia blue.

"I brought amenities." Slippers. Bathrobe. Both bespoke.

"Thanks." Syllables shiver. "For nothing."

"The Opry will fire you if they find out you drink. Not to mention what the newspapers will do. Is that what you want?"

"No."

"You're in good hands here," I say. "Dr. Wertham pioneered aversion therapy in middle Tennessee."

⌖

"How do you feel about vodka?" the doctor says.

"Hate it," Hank says, squirming. The restraints are leather.

Dr. Wertham pours. Injects. Hank bucks. Upchucks. Vodka. Gin. Blood. A Bloody Mary. Of sorts.

Hank blacks out.

⁂

"Ouch." Hank flips onto his stomach.

"Ouch." Hank flips onto his back.

He swings his legs around. Gets out of bed. Shuffles across the room. It's dark. Slippers slap.

He flips on the bathroom light. Pees. Elbows holey as needle books. His back hurts. Pain lines pour. And his ass. It feels like something's sliding out.

Why does my ass hurt? he thinks.

⁂

"Don't," Hank says. "Please."

"Little prick." Dr. Wertham sticks him with a hypo.

Hank pukes up beer. Then blood. Then air. Then blacks out.

I step from behind a curtain.

"He's vomiting sooner," Wertham says. He rolls Hank onto his side. Takes his pulse. Stethoscopes his chest. Shakes out a thermometer.

"Allow me." I stick it in Hank's rectum. Pull it out. Lick it.

"Is he hot?" the doctor says, smiling.

"You tell me." I roll Hank over so he's face-down.

"Breathtaking, isn't it?" the doctor says. "It's the Mount Rushmore of asses."

My face is in it.

❧

"That's me!" Hank says.

On the cover of *Hillbilly Fan*, a glossy. The headline: HANK'S HOT HAUTE HILLBILLY A HIT!

He's in the hospital gift shop. Crocheted
bookmarks. Fabric flowers. He takes the
magazine to the counter, shakes it at the girl.

"Recognize him?"

She looks at the photo. Then at Hank. His
colour's wan. A beard beginning. Cowlick. She
looks at the photo. Then at Hank. He's in his
robe. Pockets crammed with Kleenex.

He holds it near his face. "Now?"

"Are you lost, sir?"

He walks away. Bowlegged as a cowboy. A
pukey kewpie. Love bites for saddle sores.

CHAPTER FIVE

The backdrop's a barn.

The audience buzzes like a busted amp.

Judge Roy Hay says howdy. "Get ready, folks. Here comes the Opry's brightest star—and I do mean bright!"

Hank steps out. His suit sports a farm scene— sequinned steeds, beaded barbed wire. A creek of Austrian crystals. His guitar scuffed from rhinestones.

A standing ovation. Flashbulbs flash. Hank starts into his single *tout de suite*. I warned him.

Flashbulbs fade fine fabric.

—·—

"That's some suit," Tubb says.

I'm in the wings. I size up Tubb's ensemble.

His collar's unstable. The pants are odds.

"How's about making me a suit like that?" he

says. "Not exactly like that. I'm thinking maybe

Texas." He tips his ten-gallon. "They call me the

Texas Troubadour."

"I work exclusively for Hank." I walk away.

"What's he paying?" Tubb yells. "I'll pay

double! Triple!"

—·—

Hank and I duck out the stage door. An alley.

Flashbulbs bleach it. Girls await. They ring

Hank, wave autograph books. Pages pink and

yellow.

Hank signs. I stand to the side. Out of the heel of my eye I spy them. Boys. Near the Cadillac. Tinfoil taped to the yokes of their shirts. Duct tape piping. Boots painted orange. Their mothers' scarves around their necks.

"They're being you," I say.

"I'll be damned," says Hank.

"Well?" I say.

The store's a shell. Drywall daubed with undercoat. Dust lies deep. "What is it?" Hank says.

I direct him to a drawing tacked to drywall. HANK'S CORRAL. Letters resemble ropes. The perspective's impeccable. "Artist's conception," I say. I'm the artist.

"A store of me?" Hank is in the drawing. Standing in an aisle. Stylized, sketchy. Like people on patterns. "What do I sell?"

"Prêt-à-porter."

"Pretty poor what?"

"Clothes," I say. "Accessories. If your fans are going to dress like you, you may as well profit."

He rubs his neck. "You really think?"

⁓

"Show me something showy," Tubb says.

A men's store. Might as well be a bank. Mahogany and mirrors. Ties displayed in wickets. Dust swirls like paisley. A clerk leads Tubb to herringbones.

"No, no, no." Brown blazers flecked with grey. Grey blazers flecked with brown. He waves a page torn from *Hillbilly Fan*. Hank in Nudie. "Don't you have something like this?"

He steps outside. Empty-handed. He tries Gentry Esq. Menswear. He tries The Olde Suit Shoppe. Same story.

Then he sees it. In a store across the street. It sparkles. A suit. He dodges cars. He runs.

It's a locksmith's. The suit's a rack of keys.

"Hello, ladies," Hank says.

We're in a sweatshop. Seamstresses at chain stitch machines.

"It's done piecemeal," I say. "This woman's stitching sleeves. This one's doing cuffs. At the end of it we have these."

Mannequins model. Shirts covered in stallions, a conversational print. The print bleeds. Hank gets a spark.

"The thread count's negligible," I say. For ladies there are gauchos. "A blend." Belts are suedine. Or calftex. "The sequins are store-bought." I pinch one. It creases. "Tin. Unlike yours."

"What are mine?"

I smile. "Not tin."

—◆—

"Next," I say.

A woman steps into the atelier. She's old.

Bifocals. Boobs down to here.

"Tell me," I say, scanning her application,
"what colour would you paint the Men's
Department?"

"The colour most preferred by men is blue.
Sir." The woman twirls her lanyard.

"What is mercerized cotton?" I say.

"Lansdowne? Pongee?" I ask: How are metal
fixtures cleaned? What is a collar socket? Why is
flour paste not satisfactory on crepe paper?

I address Hank. "Do you have any questions?"

Hank shrugs. I dismiss her. The next applicant
enters. A brick shit house. Pencilled eyebrows.
Lips drawn.

Hank whispers. "Are they all ugly?"

"I'm concerned with experience and salesmanship, Hank. These applicants were the most professional."

"I know someone good," Hank says.

～⭒～

Quiet, signs say.

Hank clanks across the hospital lobby. His ensemble makes sounds. Buttons on beads.

The girl's stocking Hallmark cards. Get Well. With Sympathy.

Hank steps in, hat in hand. His Stetson's orange. To match his suit. "Recognize me?"

"You're him! I mean you!" She blushes. Cutely.

～⭒～

The sun's western. The sky dip-dyed. They cross the hospital grounds. Grass stains her

Mary Janes.

"I brought you a gift." A cloth doll. "It's me."
Clothes painted on. Sequins stitched on skin.
"It's a sample," he says. "From my store. I've
got all kinds. Clothes. Hats. Souvenirs.

"I was hoping that you might want to work
there," he says. "Whatever you're making here,
I'll pay more. Plus, you get all the dresses you
want. And tickets to the Opry."

She eyes his wedding finger. A ring of
greenish skin. A cheap band stained him. "Will
your wife be there?"

"Ex," he says. Piano. "Ex-wife. She's
divorcing me. She found some other guy. It's
just me now. Me and Nudie. He's my manager."

She giggles. "What kind of name is that?"

He giggles. "I don't know. French?"

"He loves her."

I pluck a sequin.

"He loves her not."

I pluck another. From a Hank doll. A single sequin remains. Where a nipple might be.

"That's so sweet," I say. "He loves her."

I hurl the doll. It hits a wall. Falls. Wood wool bleeds. A back-stitched seam for a spine.

Needs more sequins, I think.

⊰•⊱

I take Bobbie on a tour. That's her name. Fixtures affixed. Sconces ensconced.

"It's a dream," she says. Dude ranch decor. Chuck wagon checkout. Saloon doors swing on change rooms. A chandelier of branding irons. Dangling.

I hold the curtain. The stockroom dark with dungarees. "Your desk will be here," I say.

"That's it? No test?"

"Let's get you a uniform."

Bobbie spins before the cheval glass. A picture in a flower-incrusted bolero.

"The crowning touch." Cowboy boots appliquéd with leather flowers and glass beads. I slip them on her feet.

"I'm going to work so hard," she says. "You won't regret this."

"I know I won't," I say.

I escort her to the landing. She starts down the stairs. Her feet skate out. She flies down the flight. Ass over tea kettle. Skirt over head like a country mouse doll.

I inch down the stairs. They're slick with floor wax. I yank her boots off. Soles are leather. Slick with floor wax.

Her shin's broken. Broken through skin. I
snap off splinters of bone. Shards sharp enough
to sew sealskin. I drop them into the pockets of
my smock. Thimbles protect me.

◄━►

Bobbie's in traction.

A doctor comes in. Dr. Wertham. "A gentleman
here to see you." He holds up a hand mirror.
"Would you care to freshen up?"

She strains to sit up. Arm in a cast. Front
tooth chipped. An eye black as boldface. Bruises
are pound symbols.

"Feeling better?" Hank bounds in.

"Don't look!" She tugs the bedspread over her
head. The bedspread speaks. "I'm sorry, Hank.
You have to leave."

"When can I see you?"

"Go!"

The grass is blue. The sun, too.

Tinted windows. I'm in the Cadillac.

Hank climbs in. "I'm cursed," he says. "I have the worst luck with women."

"Then forget them," I say, gunning down the hospital's horseshoe drive.

"But I need loving!"

"This is it, Hank. Do or die. Don't disappoint me. Are you going to pursue your dream? Or are you going to moon over women?"

"No." He looks back. He can't see her. She's inside. A big blue H like a brooch on the hospital's brick.

I blanch Bobbie bones in a rolling boil.

The water boils down. See-through skin hardens on top. Gelatin. I skim it off. Spread it on a muffin tray. The tray's tiny, a doll house prop.

I slip the tray in the oven. An hour later I pull it out. When it's cool I tip the bone muffins out. Sand them. File them. Width-wise they're one thirty-second of an inch.

Voilà. Sequins.

"Howdy!" says Hank. Breast pockets smile. Fans scream. Surround the stage. It's behind Kids' Wear. Denim diapers with sanforized seats.

"We're at the grand opening of Hank's Corral," says Judge Hay, the emcee. "Why clothes, Hank?"

"I get lots of letters," Hank says. The back of his blazer a fancywork desert. Bugle beads are cactus needles. A sequinned steer's skull courtesy of Bobbie. "They say, 'Hank, we love your clothes. Where can we get some like 'em?'"

"You don't want them going naked, do you?"

"Some of them I do! For everyone else, I've made Hankwear!"

That's his segue into his new single. About window shopping.

A sleeve rips.

I'm in the stockroom. I hear well. Better than bats.

I step into the store. Skirts sold out. Shirts need sizing. Fans picked racks clean. Now they want Hank.

Fans swarm the stage, tear hanks of Hank hair. His suit. A woman bleeds from her hands. His sequins are sharp.

Vultures, I think, striding into the skirmish. Poking. Slashing. Seam ripper in hand. I always have one. A seam ripper, a needle, a vial of beads. In case Hank needs a fix.

⟶🦇⟵

Hank hobbles into the atelier. His suit denuded. Threads dangle beadless. Steel claws that once held stones.

I hand Hank a hankie.

"That was scary." He blots his brow. Blows his nose. "Thank God you got me out—" He crumples. As if boned.

"Nobody mauls Hank Williams." I yank his pants down.

His ass supple as a Stetson. The perfect crush.

⟶🦇⟵

Hank's in hospital.

"Rise and shine." Dr. Wertham slips him smelling salts.

Hank sits up. Rug burn on his belly. Tongue tacky. Chloroform does that. "I fell?"

"Shock," Dr. Wertham says.

Hank stands up. Sways. He sees spots, black and gold sequins stitched under his eyelids. He falls back to the bed, clutches his head. "I'm sick of this place," he whispers.

His headache looks like his suits.

CHAPTER SIX

prepare plaster of Paris.

"Is this going to hurt?" Hank says.

I stick straws up his nose. Carousel brand. I slap plaster on his face. Quick-drying. I rip it off. It's made a mould. Every hair. Ingrown hair. I flip him over. "I need your neck."

His underwear is paper-thin.

His ass? Museum-quality.

Beeswax bubbles.

I pour it into moulds. It hardens. Hank's head falls out.

I heat his scalp. Hand-sew a head of hair. The hair's human. Dollar an ounce. I stitch sideburns.

I stab Hank with a hot poker. Skin sizzles. Sockets. I poke in glass eyes. Black buttons for irises. I cement teeth in his mouth. The teeth are human. A canine came from Bobbie. I coat his skin with hairspray.

I hold it to the light. No light gets through.

The mark of a fine wax head.

◄━►

"Spooky," Hank says.

"Thank you," I say.

Hank's wax head. Spit and image. Skin an inch deep.

I screw the head to a skeleton. Bones of

articulated wood. I used cedar. Enemy of moths. I drape a suit on the skeleton. A suit sequinned with shape-note symbols. Squares. Stars. Etcetera.

"It's perfect," Hank says. "It's me."

"Better," I say. "Women can't hurt him." With a red pencil I vein the whites of his eyes.

"Ouch," he says.

⬩

Meantime.

"I'm the goddamned King of Country!" Tubb says.

The bartender pours him another. It's Skull's. Glasses hang like bats above the bar.

"I should be the one with the suits!" Tubb says. "I should be the one with the store!" He downs his drink. "That punk's been on the Opry how long?"

Someone slides onto a nearby stool. Tubb

sneaks a peek. She's not bad.

She's Audrey.

—🦇—

Tubb pants.

Audrey sucks his neck. Tits. Through his shirt.
She kneels. Unzips. His dick falls out. She licks.
He drops onto her bedspread. She makes a fist
around the shaft. His balls have B.O. He shoots.
Bleaches her throat. Semen sits like heartburn in
her chest.

"Hank's old lady." He hoots.

"Don't tell him yet," she says. "Let's get him
good."

—🦇—

Ernest and Audrey step into retail space.

"The till will go here," Audrey says.

A derelict dress shop. Tubb inspects. Only

racks remain. Waterfalls of wire hangers.

"We'll put the stage here," she says.

He steps into the show window, a closed back. Glass is grey with grime. He rubs away a ring. Hank's Corral across the way. Wax Hank watches from the show window there.

"Sold," he says.

❧

Stringbean bounds onstage. His band: a washboard player, a jug player, a saw player. The saw player's missing fingertips. They launch into a reel. Stringbean on gourd.

"Thank you, Stringbean," says Judge Roy Hay. "And now our old friend, the Texas Troubadour—Ernest Tubb!"

"It's a great night," Tubb says. "I've got great news. I'm opening my own store. Ernest Tubb's Record Shop.

"It's almost ready. I got more records than I even knew. I got all your favourite stars.

"And free franks!"

⚜

"What do you think of that?" Tubb says.

Hank's chording backstage. His suit: lilac mohair. He shrugs. Copycat, he thinks.

"I got a great manager." Tubb plucks at his lapel. It's brown. It's upholstery. It's the suit Audrey made for Hank. "My manager made it. She's a real beauty. Sexy. You might know her. Audrey?"

"My Audrey?" Hank says.

"You weren't man enough to keep her."

Hank swings. Ernest ducks. Opry stars haul them apart. Little Jimmy Dickens gets Ernest. Pee-Wee King has Hank.

⚜

I step from shadows.

"Mr. Nudie!" Audrey starts. In the alley.

Behind the auditorium. "What are you doing?"

I say nothing. I stare. She's shimmering in

silk. Purple as pink eye. The shirt Hank first saw

in my window.

"I'm waiting for Ernest. Ernest Tubb. A real

man."

The silhouette's shot. The satin puckers. It

hangs wrong. "You altered my creation," I say.

"Bitch."

"Who do you think you are?" says Audrey.

"Christian Dior?"

I laugh. "I'm not Christian at all."

⚜

Hank punches Ernest.

"Ignore them," I say.

He punches again. A photo of Tubb. It's pinned

to a bolt of cloth I suspended from the atelier ceiling.

"They won't last."

"How do you know?" He uppercuts. "They're laughing. At me. Right now!" He jabs. The cloth's sharp. It draws blood. Hank sucks his knuckles. "What is this stuff?"

Punchinella.

❧

"I need something special," Tubb says. "For a gift."

The saleslady shows him foxes. Ermines. Sables shiny as 78s. He's in a furrier's. Chandeliers in change rooms.

He picks up a mink. A bell rings. It's tied to the sleeve. To scare shoplifters. He peeps at the price.

"Not that special," he says.

❧

Tubb steps from the store with a mink slung over his shoulder. Fake mink. Machine-washable.

It's fur weather. Folks in fall clothes. He rounds the corner onto Broadway. His record shop's kitty-corner. Audrey's standing in the doorway. "Audrey!" he calls. "I got you something!"

She ignores him. Climbs behind the wheel of a Cadillac. Hank's Cadillac. It barrels off, black as a blindfold.

Tubb's store glows red.

🦇

Smoke singes. Flames fly. The stage kindling.

Tubb wails. It's a three-alarm. He didn't invest in alarms. Or extinguishers. He bought a glass ball of liquid retardant. He throws it. It shatters. Liquid evaporates.

Tubb masks his mouth with a hankie. His shoes stick. The floor's gummed with guano. I spread it. Guano's got methane.

Tubb tears open a crate. Records. Records sweating varnish. Bob Wills dribbles down Tubb's hand.

Mink melts.

—✦—

Audrey arrives at the atelier.

"Did he see you?" I sharpen a needle.

"How could he miss me?" She's in head-to-toe red. She kicks off her heels. Thirteens.

She unbuttons her blouse. Bra padded. Waist cinched. A surgical corset. She drops her skirt. Her legs are shaven. Her dick's pinned down in pantyhose.

She reaches under her chin. Rips off her face. It's wax. Squelch. Spirit gum stinks.

It's Dr. Wertham.

"And the real Audrey?" he says.

◆━━◆

Audrey flips through suits she sewed Hank.

She pulls down a grey one. It's suiting. He wore it to his Opry audition. Way back when.

She throws it on her sewing table. Slits seams. She pins it to Tubb's measurements. Shoulders get smaller. Sleeves get shorter. The rise rises.

She slides the suit into her Singer, drops the guide foot. Sews. Pumping her foot pedal like a pedal steel player. Her pincushion a Hank doll. His ersatz insides.

She stops.

Sirens.

◆━━◆

"That's her!" Tubb says.

Cops cuff. Recite rights.

"What's happening?" Audrey says. She's stepped onto the porch. "Ernest? Stop them!"

"Think you can double-cross me?" he says. "Think you can make me a fool?" He's jerky. A flip book cartoon. "I saw you! The whole street saw you!"

"Saw me what?"

The cops haul her down the driveway to the cruiser. Arson, mischief, unlawful entry—the charges are serious. Sentences long.

"Tell Hank he'll get his!" Tubb yells. "Jezebel! Judas!"

She can't hear him. The cruiser peels away. Wartime homes.

Hank peers into Tubb's record shop. It's scorched. "I've got to tell Nudie," he mumbles.

He heads up the alley behind the Corral.

Whack. He drops. A thug stands over him. Tire iron in hand.

"Another hit?" the thug says.

He whacks again. Something snaps. Spine. Hank's pants fill with piss.

Dr. Wertham points to trauma. Fractured ribs, vertebrae.

X-rays on a lightboard. Lungs shaped like chaps.

"Cut him open," I say. "Cut his ass, I cut you."

A wardrobe lacquered black.

I throw it open. Bats scream. Across the atelier, through french windows, into the sky. Inkblot on evening.

"Fly!" I say. Tailor from the Crypt. Couturier from the Black Lagoon. "Fly, fiends! Find him! Destroy the hand that destroyed Hank!"

◆

"Psst."

"Keep it down," Tubb says. He's in a parking lot.

The thug leans on a lamppost. Sucks a stogie. "Pleasure doing business."

Tubb hands him bills. "Now disappear. I don't—"

A noise. They look up. Bats. Hundreds. A gross of grosses. Like black bath water. Swirling. The thug's the drain.

The stogie hits the ground.

Fangs flash. The thug's cloaked head to heel. Bats stick like brooches. Wings beating. The thug floats up. A foot. A balloon in Macy's

Halloween Parade.

Bats scatter. A skeleton clatters to blacktop.

Bat shit glitters as it dries.

❧

"Operation?" Hank says.

"Dr. Wertham will cut you open," I say. My
best Rex Morgan voice. "I'll sew you up."

Hank's in his hospital bed. The Opry sent
daisies. "What about the Opry? I'm supposed to
be there!"

I roll a home record recorder to his bedside. A
Silvertone. I got it at Sears. I put a blank disc on
the turntable. I hand him a microphone. A
script.

He reads. The disc spins. It's acetate. A crystal
needle cuts it. Shavings fly. Hank's voice in
threads. They would, I think, make a nice jacket
fringe. Saddle stitching for a shirt.

They fall apart. Acetate's waterproof. Air destroys it.

⚜

The crowd claps.

Wax Hank standing on the Opry stage. "Hello friends," he says. "Hello friends. Hello friends." The needle skips.

"Hope all you folks are enjoying yourselves here at the show today. I'm awful sorry I can't be with you.

"I've got to thank all you people for wearing my clothes, visiting my Corral." The statue sports a new Nudie. Instruments incrusted. Beaded banjo. Tamboured tambourines. The guitar's strings are real, silk coated in silver.

"I had an operation. I had to. My spine needed some tuning up. It was all worn out. Maybe it's from carrying guitars. Or riding in cars. I don't know. I really thought I could be here but those are the breaks, I reckon. I sure wish I could swap this bed for that stage. I'll make it back soon. I swear. Nothing can keep Hank down for long. Bye now."

Tubb won't go.

Judge Roy Hay shoves him.

Tubb inches onstage. "I'm gonna sing a hymn tonight. About God. And sin. And forgiveness. Especially forgiveness.

"This is for Hank." Eyes on the belfry he strums his guitar. Crosses painted on his suit. A wooden crucifix dangling from his neck. A garland of garlic.

CHAPTER SEVEN

}sit front-row. It's a teaching hospital. The operating room has a balcony.

Hank's wheeled in on a gurney. Knee-high hose keep his feet from swelling. A machine measures heartbeats. Hank gets gassed.

Dr. Wertham flips him over. Pens a broken line down his back. Instruments on tissue paper. Wertham picks up the scalpel. Slits. Hank flaps open like a hospital gown.

Wertham straps a steel bar to his spine.

Now he's a judy.

Hank's facedown.

"He'll heal," Wertham says.

I stroke Hank's back. Stitches candlewicks.

"He'll need to stay off his feet for a spell. And he'll need constant care. If you'd like, I could recommend a nurse—"

"I can take care of it." I slide my hand over Hank's cheeks. They're colder than the rest of him.

"Mr. Nudie!" Bobbie says.

The gift shop reeks of Thrills. I buy gum. I need it. I necked with Hank's butt.

"I kept meaning to call Hank. Thank him for the flowers." She stares at her splint. "I felt so embarrassed. For letting him down."

"You can make it up to him." I tell her about

Hank's surgery. "He'll need help with little things," I say. "He could use someone like you to keep him company. I'll pay."

"But I'm not a nurse." Her white dress. Paper hat. "I just dress like one for the shop."

"Finding the right clothes," I say, "is half the battle."

"Special delivery," Bobbie says.

Hank wakes. Wipes crow shit off his eyes. "Bobbie?"

She has chocolate bars. Comic books, war and western. A paint-by-numbers kit of an Indian chief.

She wheels in a cart. Television on top. She plugs it in. The screen's static. She adjusts the antennas. More static, black and white, a tweed.

"Do you play crib?" she says.

⚊🦇⚊

Katy Keene can't decide what to wear. She tries on a georgette gown. A chintz. A voile. A dress in every panel. A panel in every dress.

"How can you read this junk?" Hank says.

"It's romantic," Bobbie says. She dusts. A sugar drip.

"I'd rather watch you," he says, putting down the comic. Bobbie's uniform has a bosom front, a princess back. "You're prettier than Katy."

She reddens. And you're cuter than Errol, she thinks.

Errol Swoon.

⚊🦇⚊

"Susan," Bobbie says.

"For Susan," Hank says, signing a promo photo.

Bobbie slips it in an envelope. She tears open another. "This one's from Christine."

Hank signs to her. He's sitting up in bed. In the photo he leans on a snake fence. The backdrop's a painting of the Painted Desert.

Strings span the hospital room. Fan letters hang like laundry. Postcards postmarked Ohio, Oahu, Ontario. She clothespins those. "Must be nice," she says. "Being loved."

"It'd be nice to love someone back." He puts his pen down. Charley horse.

She massages his fingers. Kisses his palm.

She tastes coin.

✦

She pulls down her panties. Fur shows.

"Wait." He rifles through the nightstand. In his wallet a safe. She slips it on. He rolls on top.

"My back," he says. "I can't."

He rolls onto his back. She climbs on top.

"Ow," he says.

She lies sidelong. He slides in. She groans. All vowels.

⟳

"How's my boy?" I say.

Dr. Wertham hands me a rubber. "I found this in his trash last night. What shall I do?"

"Not a thing." I pour in water. It runs out the other end, slicks the atelier floor. "This is perfect."

There's a tear in the tip of the rubber. I made it. With an embroidery needle. A crewel.

⟳

"Morning," Bobbie says.

"Come to bed," Hank says.

She climbs in beside him. He raises the

siderails. It's a single. She sucks his neck. His belly-button.

She swallows his sex. He moans like a recovery room. Pulls on another rubber. It's crewelled, too.

☙

Bobbie wears a garter to work. Giggling, she strips. She tosses her bra. Hank sniffs it. She tosses her hose. He puts them around his neck.

She shimmies out of panties. Goes to toss them. Spots something. Spots. In the crotch. Blood gone brown.

Uh-oh, she thinks.

☙

I'm buffing a suit with a chamois. And sawdust. Sawdust shines gemstones. The suit's new. Millionaire's cloth bejewelled with carnival rides. The Zipper.

"Bobbie paid me a visit today," Dr. Wertham says. "Her menses is late. She's spotting. Cramps." From his patch pocket he pulls a vial of blood.

I uncork it. Swish it. Sniff. "It's a child."

I sip. "A boy.

"It's Hank's.

"It's delicious."

⚜

"Pregnant," Bobbie says.

Hank sits up. Stitches strain. "You sure?"

Tears muck up her make-up. Mascara's main ingredient—guano. "We're going to have a child." She takes a stab at a smile.

He starts to cry. Softly, the way Roy Acuff cries when he sings *The Precious Jewel.* "I'm going to be a daddy," Hank says. "I'm going to be a daddy!"

He pulls a hankie from his pj's. It's warm
from his bum. I bet.

⟶🦇⟵

I act shocked.

"We didn't plan it," Hank says.

"But it's been a blessing," Bobbie says.

"I asked Bobbie to marry me," Hank says. "We
wanted you to be the first to know." He hugs her
waist. Still bedridden.

"I'm proud," I say. "I knew you'd do the
decent thing. The Christian thing." I wipe my
eye. Crying controllably. My tears are like my
shoes. Crocodile.

⟶🦇⟵

"They're darling," Bobbie says.

A little velvet suit. A little velvet dress.

Nudies. Natch. I sewed them for a midget.

We're alone. "Those are for your child," I say.
"Now, something for the bride."

She gasps. It's a wedding gown. Brodé bodice.
Illusion veil. A train's embroidered on the train.
"How'd you make it so quick?"

"Time is of the essence," I say. "You and Hank
must be wed before the press catches wind of
your condition."

"They should mind their own business," she
says.

"Welcome to showbiz," I say.

"I do," she says.

Judge Roy Hay presiding. "Do you, Hank,
take Bobbie to be your lawfully wedded wife,
in sickness and in health?"

"I do," says Hank. He's in a wheelchair. The
ceremony's onstage at the Opry. The cast cheers

from the wings.

"I now pronounce you man and wife."

Bobbie tosses the bouquet. Minnie Pearl
catches it. Bill Monroe plays *Here Comes the
Bride*. Confetti flutters. Rice. Mice scamper
under pews.

Bobbie rolls Hank down the ramp, up the aisle
of the Ryman, tin cans tied to his handlebars.
It's standing room only.

"Who are these people?" she whispers.

"Nudie sold tickets," he whispers.

———

Hank and Bobbie dance. I use the word
loosely. She spins him around in his wheelchair.

Guests cheer. Corral clerks. Opry artists.
Radio personalities. They're binging on
barbecue. Spilling sparkly.

It's the banquet hall at the Tulane Hotel. I

decorated. The centrepiece sculpted from ice. A rider on a rearing steed.

It's melting. The rider's arm drops off.

"How macabre," Dr. Wertham says.

"That's nothing," I say.

"Home sweet home," Hank says.

Bobbie wheels him into their new home, the penthouse suite at the Tulane Hotel. I rented it. "It's breathtaking."

Windows look down on downtown. The Ryman stories below. Stained glass glows like something I'd sew. "The ceremony was pretty," he says. "Don't you think it was pretty?"

"Nicest shotgun wedding ever." She winks. Cutely.

"Don't talk like that," he says. "It's like Nudie said. This kid's no accident. He's a gift." He grins. "Nudie Jr. That's what I want to call him."

"What if he's a girl?"

"Nudina."

＊

I lead Dr. Wertham into a fur vault.

He shivers. He's in his lab coat. It's thin, cut from a cloth called Indianhead. Airflow is baffled.

Jars sit on shelves. I put them up. Freak show babies. The froggy kid. The kid with a tail. A jar stands empty.

"Little Hank?" Dr. Wertham grins. "Can you imagine what a freak show will pay for that?"

"Freak shows," I say. "I'll make copies. Sell them to every sideshow in the south."

＊

Hank wheels into the atelier.

"Shouldn't you be resting?" I say.

"I've got mouths to feed now, Nudie." He dressed himself. His shirt's buttoned wrong. "What's cooking? What's up?"

I hand him a kewpie.

"It's me!" he says. It's Hank. Purple suit painted on. Tinsel glitter glued willy-nilly. A slot in the back of his head. Hank shakes his kewpie. It rattles. "How do you get the money out?"

I smash it.

"There's more where that came from," I say.

Hank towers over a carnival.

It's a miniature, a maquette. Hank's Cowboy Caravan.

"The fan mail swayed me," I say. "Not all of your fans can come to see you. So I'll take you to them."

The Fish Pond's cellophane. Fish are in scale. Spurs form a Ferris wheel. Sideshow tents the size of roach traps. A carousel spins clockwise.

"It'll be ready by spring." A stage stands behind the rides. "It'll tour clear across the country. You'll play a nightly show. During the day we'll stage rodeos. Shoot-outs. Cowboy contests."

"What about junior?" he says. "And Bobbie?"

"They'll be there," I say.

—🦇—

"Relax," Dr. Wertham says.

Bobbie drops her head to the pillow. She shifts her hips down the table. Lifts her ankles into stirrups.

He snaps on gloves. Runs a finger over genitals. Palpates her labia major, labia minor. Spreads his fingers. A victory sign. He peers into the introitis.

He inserts a steel speculum. With his dominant hand. Twists until the handle's up against her. Peers in. Cervix. Uterus. Ovaries are active. "Looks fine," he says. "No redness, swelling, dilation."

Yet. He swabs her. The swab's been dipped in arsenic. A little arsenic helps the unborn grow.

Tails. Flippers. That extra head.

⤙🦇⤚

"How's our kid?" Hank says.

"All clear," says Bobbie, dropping into bed. "You?"

"Big news. I went over to Nudie's place and—" Hank goes on.

Bobbie doesn't listen. She sees something. In his stitches. A puff of white. Pus? She pinches. Peroxides. It gets whiter.

He squirms. "Maybe Dr. Wertham should do it."

"It doesn't look like infection." She tweezes.

Pulls it out. It's white. Cloth. A label. Sewn to

skin. Design by Nudie.

◄──┬──►

"You have to say something," Bobbie says.

Hank sits. Stares. Woodgrain wallpaper.

"He doesn't own you, Hank. You're not some

suit he sewed. Friends don't sew labels into

friends!"

"Audrey," Hank mutters. "Ernest. Nudie. Why's

everyone want to hurt me?" He begins to bawl.

I'll tell Nudie what's what, she thinks. I'm

not afraid.

She thinks.

◄──┬──►

I step from the elevator.

I stop dead. My suits stacked in the hotel hallway.

Bobbie answers the door. "You're not welcome here." She's shaking. She can't look me in the eye.

"Where's Hank?"

"Hank trusted you. How can we ever trust you again?" She hands me the bloody label. "I don't know what kind of sick joke you were playing, but it's over." The door slams shut.

My eyes glow red as on-air lights. Eye teeth elongate. I grab the doorknob. It zaps me. A joy buzzer. With teeth. I can't get inside. Vampire rules. I need an invitation.

I scream. Nothing comes out. Nothing humans hear.

CHAPTER EIGHT

nise," I say.

Dr. Wertham adds anise. The brew spits. A boa of smoke. He adds senna, golden seal, oil of cloves. Paregoric, tincture of opium cut with camphor.

"The *pièce de résistance*." I hold a bat above the beaker. Drool drips from its fangs. "Hank will be back. Begging for help."

I stir in moonshine.

"He just sits there," Bobbie whispers. "And cries."

"I'll see what I can do," Dr. Wertham says. He pads into the bedroom.

Hank's in his wheelchair. He's staring out the window. Snow is a rayon warp with clipped wool tufts.

"Hank," Dr. Wertham says. "What Nudie did was abominable. But you can't let it ruin your life."

Hank says nothing.

Dr. Wertham pours out a tablespoon. "This will help."

⋙

The suite's decked out for the season. The Christmas tree is textbook. Branches buried. Mercury glass. Kugels. Silver icicles are lead. Bobbie's signing Christmas cards.

"Where is it?" Hank says.

"You can't walk!" she says.

"I don't care!" He stumbles into the room à la Frankenstein. Hankenstein. Vampire bats secrete anaesthetic saliva. He rifles through the fridge. He drains the bottle of medicine. The label says: Eidun Pharmacy.

·<·

"Thank God," Bobbie says.

Dr. Wertham steps into the suite. Hank drank the medicine. And a bottle of rubbing alcohol. And vanilla.

Hank's in the living room. He snaps a bubble light off the tree. Drains it. "Merry Christmas!" he says. He drinks down another light. It's blue. The tree darkens. He lights up.

"Hank, for the love of God." Bobbie clutches his arm. He belts her. She falls. Her head catches the coffee table. She groans, grabs her stomach.

"The baby! The precious baby!" Dr. Wertham hoists up Bobbie, hustles her out of the penthouse.

"Go!" Hank says. He stumbles after them. He pitches a kugel. "You never loved me," he says. "You or Nudie. Or Audrey. Anybody. Nobody loves me."

He spins around. Which hurts.

Hank's head lifts. His neck's rusty. Drool pooled.

He's in the bathroom. The toilet hasn't been flushed in forever. The pee's scummy. Towels sopped with puke.

He crawls down the hall. Underwear worn. He's shrinking. His ass is falling. The tree's dying. A tree skirt of dead needles.

"Help," he says.

※

Fiddlin' Arthur Smith's onstage. Fiddling.

Ernest Tubb's tuning up. He's dressed in a Santa suit. Bats wouldn't hurt Santa, he thinks. Would they?

It's the Christmas show. *Le tout* Opry is backstage. The Fruit Jar Drinkers. The Skillet Lickers. The Gully Jumpers.

Hank staggers in. Worse for wear. His suit's store-bought. Smells like something crawled inside and died. He drops at the feet of Judge Roy Hay.

His breath's nice. He's been drinking perfume.

※

I'm shaving a suit. Purple pills.

Wertham walks in. "Hank," he says. "He's left

the hotel."

"Not to worry." I clap hands. A bat swoops to my shoulder. Pirates have parrots. I hold up the sleeve of the suit. The bat sniffs. "Find Hank," I say.

"No need," Wertham says. "I know where he went. He's drying out. Judge Hay checked him into the hospital. Baptist Hospital."

The bat hisses.

"He's out of my reach, Nudie."

I smile. I blow lint from my blade.

Hank: "Zzzzzzzz."

Judge Roy Hay: "Get up."

Hank jerks. Baptist Bible by his bed. Baptist cross overhead. The window treatment is vile.

"I got this today." The Judge tosses Hank a manila envelope. "So did our sponsors."

Hank tears it open. Out slide snapshots. Of himself. A dick in his mouth. His ass getting eaten. His ass getting fucked. The fucker's me.

"They want you gone," the Judge says. "So do I."

—◆—

Hank tries the knob. Locked.

He swills rye. Cries out. Smashes door glass with his elbow. Reaches in. Unbolts the deadbolt.

He limps into the atelier. I'm not there. The suits I sewed for him are standing around. I stuffed them with stiff white tissue. Posed them. Hank sucking Hank. Hank fucking Hank fucking Hank.

He grabs the rod from the steamer. Swings. Suits cave. Tissue leaks from sleeves and necks.

Ectoplasmically.

—◆—

"Nudie?"

The door breaks down. Hank stumbles into the Corral. It's closed. I'm not there.

Wax Hank is. He's naked. And anatomically correct. Dick, balls. Hair runs up his ass crack like weeds run down country roads.

"Son of a bitch!" He grabs the store's clothes steamer. Drops it. Lightning bolts shoot from his spine. He reaches into his coat. The rye's almost gone. A heel. Backwash.

He hurls it at boots. Gasping, he stumbles over to the souvenirs and snatches up a snow dome. Snow squalls around a statuette of Hank. He uncorks the dome, drinks it dry. He drinks another. He's getting warmed up.

⚓

Hank wanders up the midway. It's being built. Wind whistles through stalls of penny whistles.

112

I step out of the Haunted House.

"I knew you'd be here," he says. The shine's off the apparel. Boots shedding snakeskin.

"You look like hell, Hank."

"You're going to hell," he says.

"You wanted to be a star. I dressed you like a star. What will happen when I stop dressing you?"

"You're a sick, twisted pervert, Nudie."

The Marquis de Sawdust. "I can make you immortal, Hank. Wouldn't you like to live forever?"

"I should have done this a long time ago." He pulls a pistol from his pocket. Cocks it. He pukes blood. The reddest ink. He drops to his knees. Stars are spurs.

🦇

Dr. Wertham's waiting at the hospital.

I park. Hank's splayed across the back seat.

"A touch too much tincture?" Dr. Wertham
says.

I punch in the cigarette lighter. It pops out.
Red-hot. I press it to Hank's hand. It sizzles.
Burns a circle. No H. Skin stinks.

CHAPTER
NINE

hearse crawls up Commerce.

Past Ernest Tubb's Record Shop. Gospel's a specialty.

Past Hank Snow's Music Shop. Guitars hang by their necks.

Past Roy Acuff's Haberdashery. He sells silk ties he paints himself. With cacti. Lassos. Horses are moving well.

⌐•═══•⌐

I'm standing outside the Opry. The street's

shut down. Sawhorses block parking stalls.
Shopping bags hood meters.

I walk up Fifth. Newsies hawk papers. Hank's
the scarehead. Dead at twenty-nine. Heart
attack, alcohol-induced.

A man's selling swatches. Cut, he claims, from
Hank's clothes. A busker sings Hank's songs. He
stands outside the liquor store. Guitar case open.
He's grossed seven cents.

I throw him a quarter. He stares at me and
sings. He's prettier than Hank. Lashes bat. His
suit's shoddy, cuffs ragged as wedding
invitations.

"Thanks, friend," he says, finishing. "I'm
Johnny Horton."

⚊🦇⚊

Hank Snow sings *Beyond the Sunset.*
Roy Acuff sings *Peace in the Valley.*

A church choir sings next. *My Record Will Be There*. The audience joins in. The Ryman's hung with black bunting.

Judge Roy Hay steps onstage. He reads from the Bible. Hank's casket's open. Guitars made of carnations stand sentry at each end. Immortelles, they're called.

⎯🦇⎯

Johnny paws Hank's suits.

I light a smoke. Fabric sucks it up. "Try one on."

He strips. A moth flees his garments. He dons Hank's Desert Suit. He's drowning in it. He poses in the mirror. "I always dreamed of wearing a suit like this," he says.

I pluck the moth from midair. Eat it. It tastes like wool. "You know what you need?" I say. "Cologne." From my pocket I pull a cut-crystal bottle. It's Stetson-shaped. "Eau de Gringo."

Johnny sniffs it.

Chloroform. He drops. The rectum's full of veins. Hence hemorrhoids. I sink my teeth into his ass. O negative!

◄❉►

Dr. Wertham escorts Bobbie to the bier. She's showing. She sobs. Strokes Hank's face.

Skin breaks. Her hand slips into his skull.

He's wax. He gets under her nails. She shrieks.

Judge Roy Hay clears the stage. He signals security. "Find him, goddammit! Find Hank!"

CHAPTER TEN

ohnny just came to.

"I'm Dr. Wertham," Dr. Wertham says.

Johnny's eyes adjust. He's in a hospital room. In a hospital bed. The hospital gown suits him. He's a winter.

"You suffered a small mishap," the doctor says. "A reaction to the cologne. I'm afraid you're allergic to lavender."

"Mr. Nudie must think I'm an idiot."

"On the contrary," the doctor says. "He left you this."

A snow dome. Johnny's in it. Mini-Johnny.
Playing the guitar. The Ryman's the
background. "Wow," he says. He shakes it. Snow
squalls stir. "How'd he do this?"

The statue is plaster. The liquid is antifreeze.
Snow's made of bone chips.

Hank's bones. Hank snow.